THE PEACE-AND-QUIET DINER
To librarians, parents, and teachers:

The Peace-and-Quiet Diner is a Parents Magazine READ ALOUD Original — one title in a series of colorfully illustrated and fun-to-read stories that young readers will be sure to come back to time and time again.

Now, in this special school and library edition of *The Peace-and-Quiet Diner,* adults have an even greater opportunity to increase children's responsiveness to reading and learning — and to have fun every step of the way.

When you finish this story, check the special section at the back of the book. There you will find games, projects, things to talk about, and other educational activities designed to make reading enjoyable by giving children and adults a chance to play together, work together, and talk over the story they have just read.

For a free color catalog describing Gareth Stevens' list of high-quality books, call 1-800-341-3569 (USA) or 1-800-461-9120 (Canada).

Parents Magazine READ ALOUD Originals:

Golly Gump Swallowed a Fly
The Housekeeper's Dog
Who Put the Pepper in the Pot?
Those Terrible Toy-Breakers
The Ghost in Dobbs Diner
The Biggest Shadow in the Zoo
The Old Man and the Afternoon Cat
Septimus Bean and His Amazing Machine
Sherlock Chick's First Case
A Garden for Miss Mouse
Witches Four
Bread and Honey
Pigs in the House
Milk and Cookies
But No Elephants
No Carrots for Harry!
Snow Lion
Henry's Awful Mistake
The Fox with Cold Feet
Get Well, Clown-Arounds!
Pets I Wouldn't Pick
Sherlock Chick and the Giant
    Egg Mystery
Cats! Cats! Cats!

Henry's Important Date
Elephant Goes to School
Rabbit's New Rug
Sand Cake
Socks for Supper
The Clown-Arounds Go on Vacation
The Little Witch Sisters
The Very Bumpy Bus Ride
Henry Babysits
There's No Place Like Home
Up Goes Mr. Downs
Bicycle Bear
Sweet Dreams, Clown-Arounds!
The Man Who Cooked for Himself
Where's Rufus?
The Giggle Book
Pickle Things
Oh, So Silly!
The Peace-and-Quiet Diner
Ten Furry Monsters
One Little Monkey
The Silly Tail Book
Aren't You Forgetting Something, Fiona?

Library of Congress Cataloging-in-Publication Data

Maguire, Gregory.
    The Peace-and-Quiet Diner / by Gregory Maguire ; pictures by David Perry.
        p. cm. -- (Parents magazine read aloud original)
    Summary: Lester worries that his life is not adventurous enough for his visiting Auntie June, but the diner where they meet offers plenty of activity after all.
    ISBN 0-8368-0971-8
    [1. Animals--Fiction. 2. Stories in rhyme.] I. Perry, David, 1946- ill. II. Title. III. Series.
    [PZ8.3.M273Pe 1993]
    [E]--dc20   93-7770

This North American library edition published in 1994 by Gareth Stevens Publishing, 1555 North RiverCenter Drive, Suite 201, Milwaukee, Wisconsin 53212, USA, under an arrangement with Parents Magazine Press, New York.

Text © 1988 by Gregory Maguire. Illustrations © 1988 by David Perry. Portions of end matter adapted from material first published in the newsletter *From Parents to Parents* by the Parents Magazine Read Aloud Book Club, © 1989 by Gruner + Jahr, USA, Publishing; other portions © 1994 by Gareth Stevens, Inc.

Printed in the United States of America

1 2 3 4 5 6 7 8 9 99 98 97 96 95 94

THE PEACE AND QUIET DINER

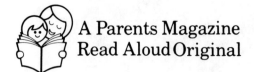

A Parents Magazine
Read Aloud Original

THE PEACE AND QUIET DINER

Story by Gregory Maguire
Pictures by David Perry

GARETH STEVENS PUBLISHING · MILWAUKEE

PARENTS MAGAZINE PRESS · NEW YORK

For Maureen Vecchione—G.M.
To Sue and Nicholas
with special thanks to
Mary Faulconer—D.P.

Lester got a letter
From his Auntie June.
She said she'd come to visit
That very afternoon.
That was very soon.

Lester knew his Auntie well.
She was full of bounce.
She always said, "Don't bore me!
Adventure is what counts!
In very large amounts!"

Lester had a photo
Of Auntie on the Nile.
She was playing tug-of-war
With a crocodile.
She had the larger smile.

Lester had a worry.
Auntie might be bored.
So he called up Morris.
"Help me, friend!" he roared.

Morris said to Lester,
"Don't have a single care.
We'll go out to eat.
Your aunt can meet us there."

The friends met at a diner.
Morris said, "What's wrong?"
Lester said, "My Auntie June
Soon will come along!"

16

"Auntie loves adventure!
She is not like us!
My life is very simple,
But Auntie loves a fuss!"

17

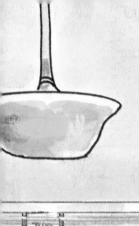

The waiter took their order,
Soup and eggs and cheese.
Lester dropped his napkin.
He said, "Excuse me, please."

When he went to find it
Down upon the floor
Morris saw some lions
Enter with a roar!

Lester got his sweater
Caught upon the chair.
Morris didn't notice.
All he did was stare.

Morris looked around him.
The place was getting busy.
So *many* folks arriving!
It almost made him dizzy.
In came seven monkeys
Swinging on the lights.
They were dressed in capes
And fancy sequinned tights.

Then a cat came selling
Raffle tickets, cheap.
"First prize is a trip," she said,
"On the ocean deep!"

Morris had some money,
So he ordered two.
"One for me," he said,
"And Lester, one for you."
The cat went springing off
When a dog began to bark.
Morris saw it all.
Lester just saw dark.

Morris said to Lester,
"This diner is a find!"
Lester didn't listen.
He just looked out the blind.

"Nothing ever happens.
I'm sure that Auntie June
Will find it very boring.
She'll be arriving soon."

Morris watched a rhino
with a feathered hat
Start to sing an opera.
(She sang a little flat.)
The monkeys did athletics.
The lions roared for more.
The rhino did a little dance
That almost broke the floor.

Lester said, "She's coming!"
Said Morris, "Don't despair!
If you'd only keep your eyes peeled
you wouldn't even care—
There's adventure everywhere!"

Auntie June was floating
In her private parachute.
She landed by the diner
In her best safari suit.

The minute that she entered
Everyone began to eat.
"Lester *darling*!" cried his Auntie.
"What a *boring* place to meet!"

Lester only whimpered.
Morris said, "Not so!
This place is fairly hopping!"
Auntie June said, "Oh?"

Just then the cat announced
It was time to have the draw.
She pulled the winning ticket
And she held it in her paw.
"The number is," she read aloud,
"Four hundred forty nine."
Everybody checked, and then
Lester cried, "That's mine!"

"A week's vacation sailing
Upon the deep blue sea!"
The cat shook hands with Lester.
Lester said, "For me?"

He stood up on the table.
He said, "This afternoon
I want to give my prize
to my lovely Auntie June!"

Auntie danced with pleasure.
Auntie was delighted.
She ran off to pack her trunk,
She was that excited.

Lester sat and smiled.
He said, "I must agree.
Adventure's all around you.
You only have to see!"

Notes to Grown-ups

Major Themes

Here is a quick guide to the significant themes and concepts at work in *The Peace-and-Quiet Diner:*

- Observation: it pays to notice your surroundings; they may be more exciting than you think!
- Special relationships: good friends can help people get through difficult times.

Step-by-step Ideas for Reading and Talking

Here are some ideas for further give-and-take between grown-ups and children. The following topics encourage creative discussion of *The Peace-and-Quiet Diner* and invite the kind of open-ended response that is consistent with many contemporary approaches to reading, including Whole Language:

- Lester was completely unaware of everything going on around him. He was too worried about something over which he had no control to enjoy the craziness of the diner. If a child is bored, he or she sometimes focuses on the boredom itself and not on what can be done to remedy it. The goal, then, is to redirect his or her attention. Can your child suggest a way for Morris to help Lester see what is occurring in the diner? That suggestion might be a key to what your own child might require when boredom strikes.
- Lester has a good friend in Morris. When Lester is in trouble, Morris is there to help. What makes a relationship special? Maybe there's a common interest, or an individual is simply fun to be with. Your child may have reasons why certain people are important to him or her. Ask your child to share those reasons with you.

Games for Learning

Games and activities can stimulate young readers and listeners alike to find out more about words, numbers, and ideas. Here are more ideas for turning learning into fun:

Adventure Book

In *The Peace-and-Quiet Diner*, Lester says to his friend, Morris: "Adventure's all around you. You only have to see!" Encouraging a child to see the possibilities for stories in the world around us is one positive way to prepare youngsters for life's adventures.

One way to do this is to help your child make his or her own Adventure Book. Look through old magazines for glossy pictures of places he or she would like to go, animals she or he might meet, and vehicles to travel in. Help your child cut out the pictures. Then together you can sort out and paste them on stiff paper that you have labeled PLACES, ANIMALS, and VEHICLES. Punch three holes along the left margin of the papers and tie the pages together with three pieces of yarn, or place all the pages in a three-ring binder. Encourage your child to tell you about what might happen if she or he went to a PLACE pictured in the book by traveling in a VEHICLE from the vehicle pages, and met an ANIMAL from the animal section of the Adventure Book. How would he or she feel when traveling in the vehicle? Would the ride be bumpy or smooth, fast or slow? What would your child do when face-to-face with the animal? What would the animal do when face-to-face with your child? How would each of them feel? Encourage different choices each time you do this book together, and add more pages when you get new magazines.

About the Author
GREGORY MAGUIRE has had lots of adventures. He's been charged by a bull elephant in Africa, has crossed a river by canoe in Central America, and has driven on expressways during rush hour. But he is nonetheless very fond of peace and quiet, wherever it can be found.

Mr. Maguire is the author of fantasy and science fiction novels for young readers. He lives in Massachusetts.

About the Artist
DAVID PERRY is very fond of both animals and diners. But although he enjoyed drawing *The Peace-and-Quiet Diner*, he wouldn't want to eat at a place like that. "Those animals would be too noisy, even for me," he says.

Mr. Perry's animals have appeared in numerous books and magazines. He is an award-winning designer/illustrator who splits his time between New York and a farm in Pennsylvania.